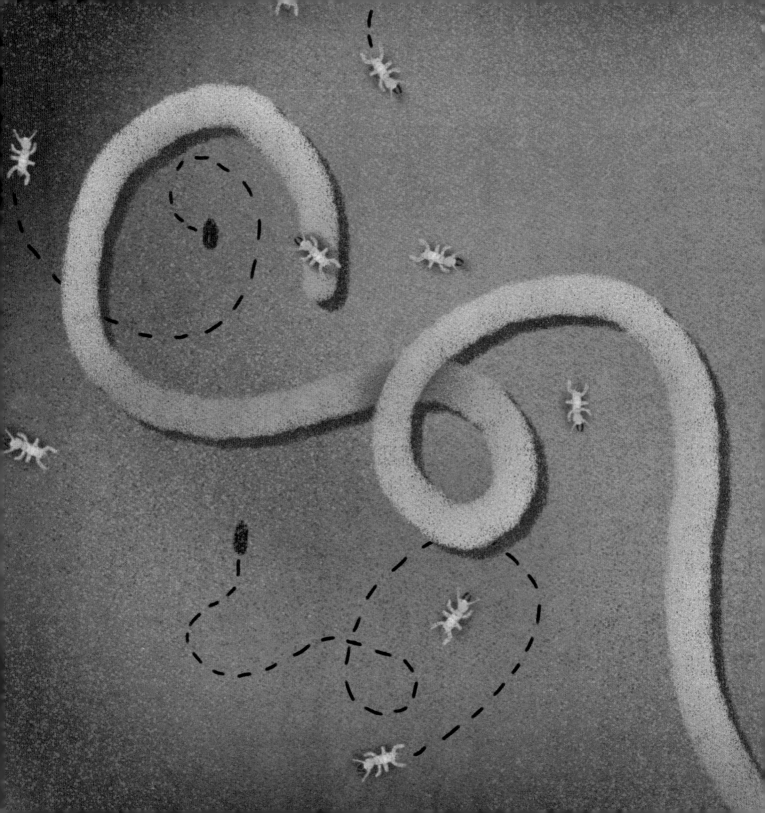

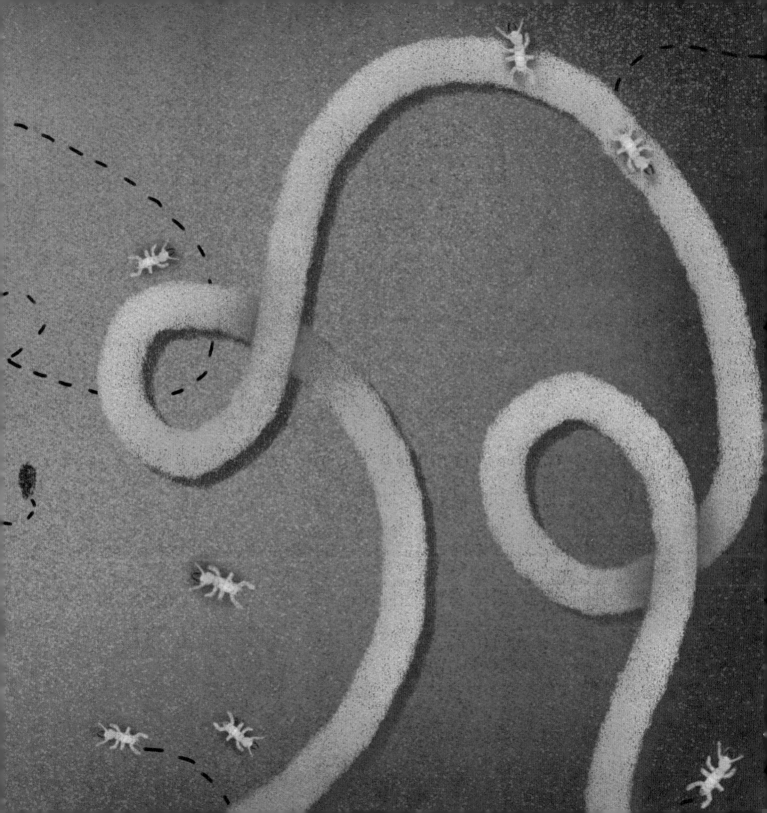

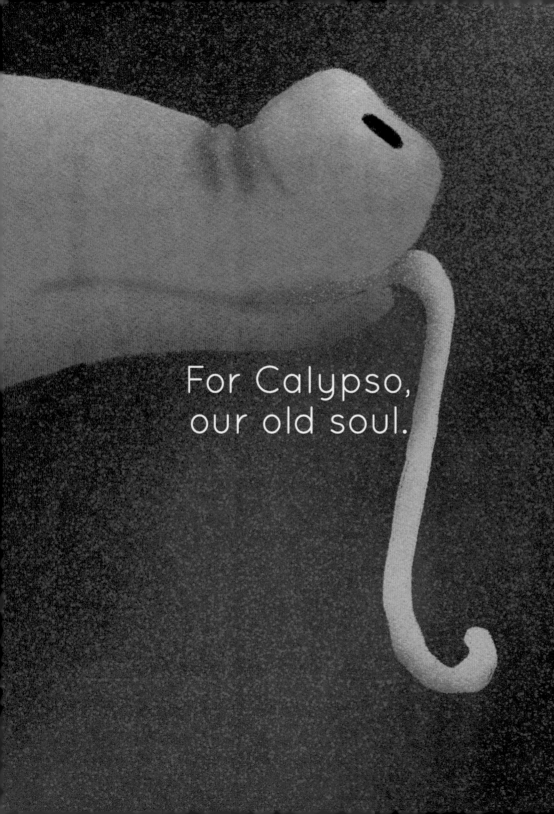

For Calypso,
our old soul.

AZYBO
the Aardvark

Written by: L.L. Eaton
Illustrated by: C.P. River

Azybo the aardvark stretched as he woke up to a cold chill, the warmth of the African day fading as night took over. His mother had left two days ago so Azybo was grown now and needed to learn to take care of himself!

Azybo didn't want to leave his mother's burrow. However, he had eaten the last of the aardvark cucumbers that were poking through the ceiling and he felt his tummy growling.

With a slight grumble, Azybo made his way through the tunnel that led out of his mother's burrow and carefully poked his long snout into the cool night air. He sniffed, listened, and cautiously looked about like his mother had taught him to.

After waiting for what felt like the right amount of time and not sensing anything dangerous, Azybo took his first steps outside the burrow without his mother by his side.

It was weird, he thought it would be scary, but Azybo wasn't frightened at all, he was excited and hungry! The cucumbers he had eaten were a great special snack, but they didn't fill him up like a nice juicy mound of termites would.

So, with food on his mind, Azybo cautiously set out into the savannah.

Being as careful as his mother had taught him, Azybo darted from one bit of cover to the next, using scrub brush, trees, and brush piles to move across the desert-like, African savannah.

It didn't take long for his big snout to catch the familiar scent of a termite mound. Following the tantalizing smell, he powered toward the giant mound and as he got closer he could hear the termites within.

Azybo didn't realize just how hungry he was until this exact moment. Without even thinking about it, he lunged forward with his powerful front arms and claws and began to dig into the termite mound like he had seen his mother do so many times.

Azybo's long, sticky tongue whipped forward into the hole he had dug and snatched up the swarming termites. They tasted amazing! He ate until he couldn't eat anymore.

With a full tummy, Azybo looked
around and noticed the moon was just
barely above a nearby baobab tree,
the night was halfway over!

Azybo needed to find a burrow to
sleep in for the upcoming day and
with that in mind, he lumbered back
out into the savannah.

Using his nose and ears more than his eyes, he searched for a hole that seemed the right size for him.

The hoot of an owl overhead startled him. He looked up, frightened, and nearly walked right into a hole!

The hole seemed the right size, so Azybo cautiously clambered into the tunnel.

The tunnel wasn't very long and when Azybo reached the small living area of the burrow he was startled to find somebody already there curled up and fast asleep.

It was a pair of fennec foxes! Azybo was nervous, he was much larger than them, but still, he didn't want a fight.

So, as quietly and quickly as he could, he backed out of the burrow.

Azybo continued his search, being more careful about checking potential burrows for signs of occupancy. He asked a cape hare for some help, but they just cackled and sprinted away into the night.

He met a nice pair of pangolins on his journey. They poked their heads out of a tunnel he was sniffing and let him know it was already occupied. They were very kind and told him about a few tunnels not far away that they thought might even have some aardvark cucumbers in them!

Daytime was dangerously close though, so Azybo had to hurry up.

He found what he thought might be one of the tunnels the pangolins had mentioned, but he was determined to be more careful inspecting this one before he climbed into it.

He was so focused on inspecting
the burrow that he didn't hear the
quiet pitter-patter or smell the
strong odor of the hyena quietly
stalking toward him.

Just as the hyena got within attack range of Azybo, a strong wind blew in the right direction and that pungent hyena odor went right up his powerful snout.

Immediately Azybo realized the mistake he made and blindly kicked behind him with his large claws. They connected with the hyena's muzzle!

Azybo scurried quickly into the tunnel.

He turned and looked at the entrance, fearing
the hyena was right behind him. He relaxed
when he realized the tunnel was far too small
for the hyena to fit through. Azybo continued
down to the living chambers.

He looked around the living chamber he was sitting in. It was comfortably sized and felt similar to the burrow he and his mother had shared.

Azybo looked up at the ceiling and saw the familiar roots of aardvark cucumbers and smiled.

As Azybo laid down to sleep, he thought about his night. It had been long, eventful, and a little scary, but overall it had been a great night and he couldn't wait to see what adventure tomorrow would bring!

Facts about aardvarks!

-Aardvarks are mammals found throughout sub-Saharan Africa! That means anywhere south of the Sahara.

-Aardvarks have a long snout and a pig-like nose. They also have rabbit-like ears and a tail similar to a kangaroo's. But they're actually their own species and not closely related to any of those other animals or any animals alive today!

-Aardvarks sleep in underground burrows.

-Aardvarks are nocturnal, which means they sleep during the day. This helps them avoid the harsh African heat!

-An aardvark can close off the large nostrils of its nose to keep out dust and insects!

-An aardvark's large ears provide a keen sense of hearing, helping them to detect predators approaching!

-An aardvark's oversized snout doesn't just look funny, it's the most powerful sniffer in the whole animal kingdom!

-An aardvark's tongue can be up to a foot long(30.5 centimeters). Not only is it long, but it's sticky too, which makes licking up termites easy!

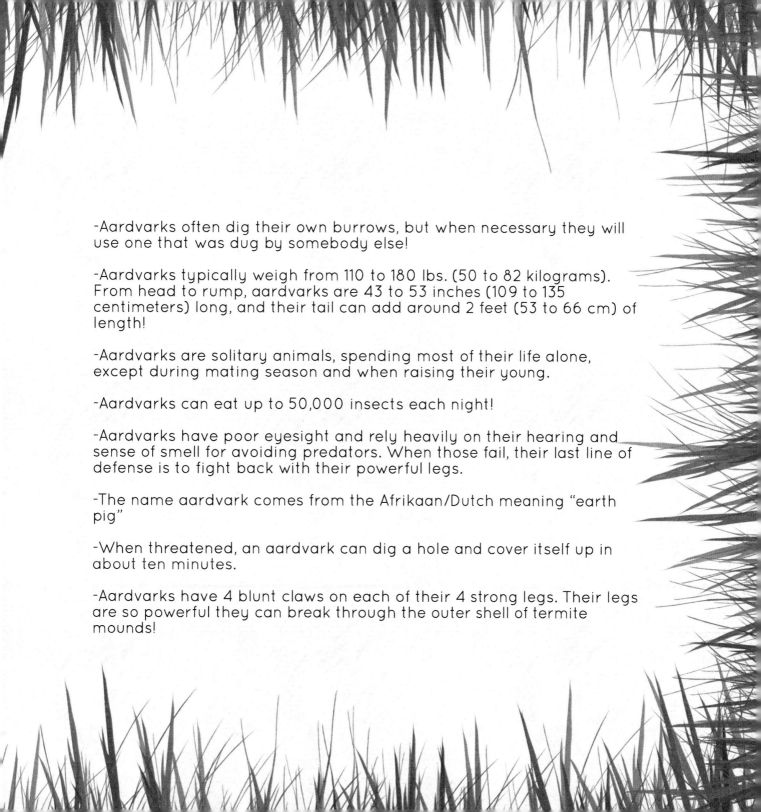

-Aardvarks often dig their own burrows, but when necessary they will use one that was dug by somebody else!

-Aardvarks typically weigh from 110 to 180 lbs. (50 to 82 kilograms). From head to rump, aardvarks are 43 to 53 inches (109 to 135 centimeters) long, and their tail can add around 2 feet (53 to 66 cm) of length!

-Aardvarks are solitary animals, spending most of their life alone, except during mating season and when raising their young.

-Aardvarks can eat up to 50,000 insects each night!

-Aardvarks have poor eyesight and rely heavily on their hearing and sense of smell for avoiding predators. When those fail, their last line of defense is to fight back with their powerful legs.

-The name aardvark comes from the Afrikaan/Dutch meaning "earth pig"

-When threatened, an aardvark can dig a hole and cover itself up in about ten minutes.

-Aardvarks have 4 blunt claws on each of their 4 strong legs. Their legs are so powerful they can break through the outer shell of termite mounds!

Facts about aardvark habitat!

-Aardvark cucumbers, also known as aardvark pumpkins have vines that grow up to 22 feet (6.7 meters) long!

-Even though Africa has an average high of 100 degrees Fahrenheit(38 degrees Celsius), at night the temperature plummets as low as 25 degrees Fahrenheit(-4 degrees Celsius)!

-Termite mounds are more than just a pile of dirt. They have heating and cooling ducts built in, are strong enough for an elephant to stand on, and will often outlast the colony of termites that built it. It's crazy to think that tiny insects build them!

-The baobab tree is iconic for Africa. It became known as 'the tree of life' because it produces nutrient dense fruit even in the dry season when water is scarce!

-Without aardvarks to eat and spread the seeds of the aardvark cucumber, the plant would die out. This is one of the many reasons the aardvark is considered a keystone species!

-The aardvark cucumber is a subterranean fruit, meaning the fruit actually forms and grows underground!

Facts about
other African wildlife!

-Verreaux's eagle-owl is the largest of Africa's owls, measuring 26 inches(66 cm) tall. It has bright pink eyelids, something no other species of owl has!

-Weighing in between 2 and 3 pounds (0.9 to 1.4 kilograms) fennec foxes are the smallest of all canids. They are 14 to 16 inches (35.6 to 40.6 centimeters) long, with another 7 to 12 inches (18 to 30 centimeters) of tail. Perhaps their most notable characteristic is their ears, which can grow to between 4 to 6 inches (10.2 to 15.2 centimeters) in length!

-The cape hare is a species native to Africa that can run at speeds of up to 45 MPH(77 KM/H) and can bound 8 feet forward and almost 8 feet high!

-Pangolins are the only mammals covered in scales!

-A pangolin's tongue is longer than its whole body. They store their tongue deep in their chest cavity when it's not in use snatching insects!

-Spotted hyenas, also known as laughing hyenas, are incredibly intelligent and often live upwards of twenty years in the wild!

-Spotted hyena are actually incredibly talented hunters, despite their reputation for being scavangers.

-Spotted hyenas have incredibly strong jaws and teeth. They can break through all the bones of their prey with just a crunch!

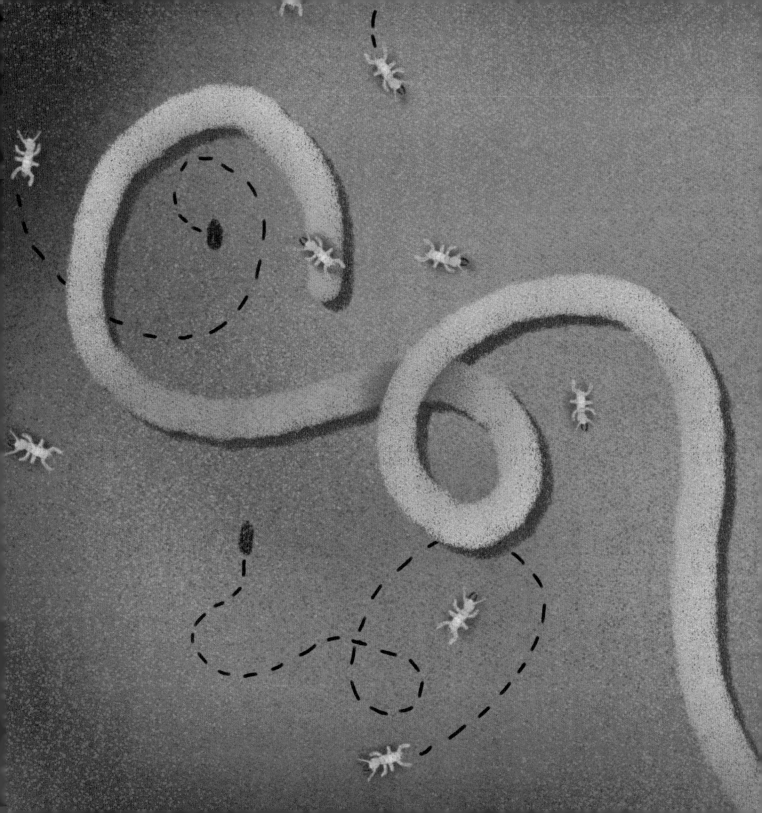

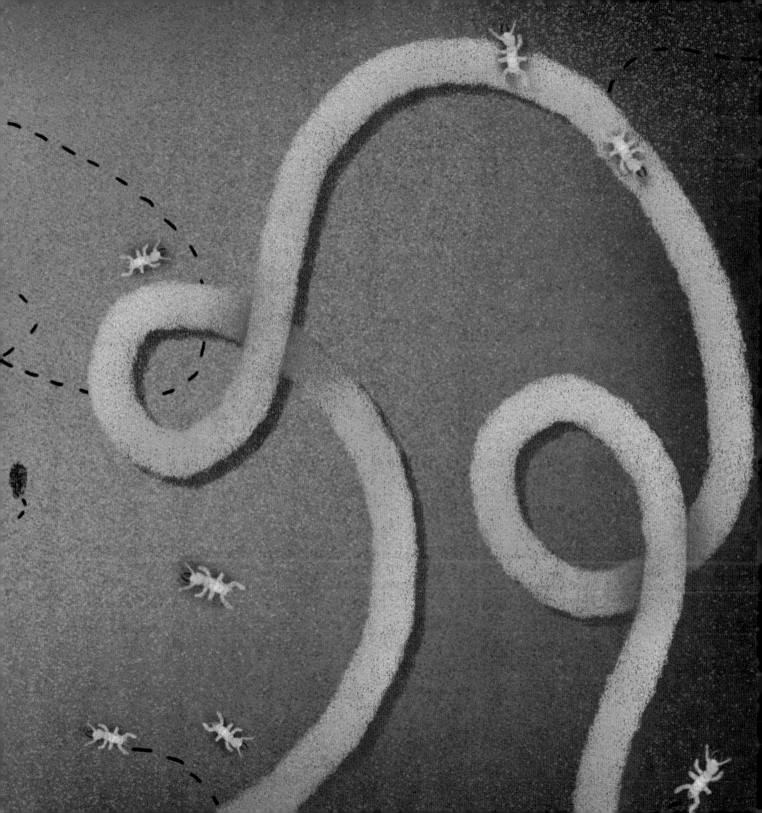

Made in the USA
Monee, IL
25 January 2023

26125790R00029